If, by telling tales, I could ...... lost and destroyed, I could ...... my imagination.
—**Günter Grass**

White Carnations is a collection of 101 tales about Syria's Civil War, its citizens, its victims, and its refugees. Sometimes vividly, often subtly, these short sketches convey to the reader the pain and the horror of the fighting in Syria and its effect on the Syrian people.
  —Arthur G. Goldschmidt, *A Concise History of the Middle East*

A brilliant translation of the highly impressive tales of Syrian novelist and poet Dr Musa Rahum Abbas. These tales bring the horrors of the war in Syria chillingly to life, and show how literature in a few striking words can convey a shocking message that penetrates. The news media is superficial by comparison.
  —Nikolaos van Dam, *The Struggle for Power in Syria*

These powerful tales by Musa Rahum Abbas are evocative and often haunting. They capture the personal, and less covered, aspects of Syria's tragedy. In this eloquent and faithful English translation, the voice of Musa Abbas will prove difficult to forget.
  —Omar Imady, *The Gospel of Damascus*

In *White Carnations* Syrian poet, novelist, and professor Musa Rahum Abbas offers us 101 page-long prose poems that speak of Syrians' heartbreak with more eloquence than newspaper or television reports can ever equal. These poems are broken shards of the broken country Syria now is—with its millions of broken people—after ten years of an unwinnable revolution that has not yet ended.
  —Frederic Hunter, *Kivu*

To my grandchildren:
Sarah, Musa, and Lima

This is the legacy of our nation, handed to you.

White Carnations reminds us why literature has a power that facts, figures, and multimedia never will have. This collection of tales uncovers the truth of war as it is understood by the only ones to whom it genuinely matters. It does so without reminding the reader of the number of dead, or the state of politics, or manipulating images of rotting corpses. Instead it tenderly highlights the simplest moments for those who survive to still walk in the wreckage. In doing so the collection shines a light on the hopes, needs, and desires of every human being.

—Marream Krollos, *Big City*

White Carnations

101 Tales of War-Torn Syria
Musa Rahum Abbas

Translated from Arabic by
Sanna Dhahir
Musa Al-Halool

 Cune

White Carnations:
101 Tales of War-Torn Syria
by Musa Rahum Abbas
© 2022 Musa Rahum Abbas
Cune Press, Seattle 2022
First Edition

Paperback   ISBN 9781951082024

Library of Congress Cataloging-in-Publication Data
Names: 'Abbas, Musá Rahum, author. | Halul, Musá, translator. |
Dhahir, Sanna, 1950- translator.
Title: White carnations : 101 tales of war-torn Syria / Musa Abbas ;
translated from Arabic by Musa Al-Halool & Sanna Dhahir.
Other titles: Buruq 'alá thuqub sawda'. English
Description: Seattle : Cune Press, 2022. | Includes bibliographical
references and index.
Identifiers: LCCN 2017004638 (print) | LCCN 2017007506 (ebook) | ISBN
9781951082024 (pbk. : alk.
paper) | ISBN 9781614572091 (Kindle) | ISBN 9781614572107 (eBook)
Subjects: LCSH: Syria--History--Civil War, 2011---Fiction. |
Syria--History--Civil War, 2011---Refugees--Fiction.
Classification: LCC PJ7902.B35 W4813 2017 (print) | LCC PJ7902.B35 (ebook) |
DDC 892.7/37--dc23
LC record available at https://lccn.loc.gov/2017004638

Bridge Between the Cultures (a series from Cune Press)

Syria Crossroads (a series from Cune Press)

Cune   Cune Press: www.cunepress.com | www.cunepress.net

Contents

I

She said, "Tell me about love, and don't stop even if I fall asleep."

Tallying

WHILE THE NEWS anchor was announcing victory and the cessation of hostilities in a country that was once full of life, the streets had been emptied of pedestrians.

Haj Abdullah took to counting who was left of his family: Muhammad perished under torture; Okba became a mujahed and joined Abul-Bara Battalion; his son Ali was blown to pieces by an explosive barrel; Said was killed while serving the flag—as it is called here.

Simo, his *crazy* grandson, counted his fingers and was immensely delighted to find that each hand had five; little Hammoudi was completely absorbed in counting his toys and strips of gum, with a cry-like smile on his face; the birds continued their ceaseless battering of the cracked pane on the opposite window.

Faces and Silhouettes

THE CAFÉ WAS ENVELOPED IN A CLOUD of smoke and sweat, along with the clamor of customers.

He was half awake and half asleep, slyly resting on his little table. Voices and pictures were racing in his foggy head: here is Happy-Go-Lucky Abboudi, with his beautiful voice singing a song by Nazem Al-Ghazali; and here is One-Eyed Hassan, The Telltale—a nickname he truly deserves—whose snitching had often earned us a beating from the teacher; and here comes Krue Kut, The Carpetbagger—he, too, deserves his nickname—he used to save his food until the second break, then take advantage of our hunger and sell us a bite or a single chickpea for whatever piasters we had.

When the smoke partially cleared, slowly defining the patrons of the café, he guffawed his usual guffaw, as his head spun sarcastically. Abboudi is now Sheikh Abdul-Kareem, the imam of the mosque; One-Eyed Hassan is now Colonel Hassan of Branch 222; Krue Kut is now Haj Muhsin, the notorious drug trafficker. His head was still foggy amid a newly forming cloud.

An Inventory

BECAUSE HE had studied business management and accounting, he inventoried everything that crossed his mind and assessed it in terms of gain or loss.

The night too was dying, and on his window pane raindrops were whispering something like tears: thirty, forty, fifty years. In his little book he jotted down addresses that might adjust those numbers, more or less. Gain in green, loss in red.

As dawn loomed, and sun rays flooded his old notebook and the deadly stillness of his cold room, red reigned supreme over lines, pages, and punctuation. What an inventory!

The Smuggler

THE RED-HAIRED, squinty-eyed customs officer took note of his unease, the slight tremor in his fingers, and the sweat on his forehead.

Very politely he asked him to wait until he had completely finished the business at hand. While his eyes were scanning the place, from the borders to the east to the blue horizon beyond the sea, he was going over English words he had learned during his college days.

The officer approached him and asked, "What are you hiding, Sir? You carry nothing but this little bag!" After some hesitation, he answered, "Under my remaining fingernails I am hiding a pinch of earth from my village. If you wish to confiscate it, then you have to pull out my fingernails—just as they did there in the detention center."

The Cell

O N MY FIRST DAY of solitary confinement, the place was cold and musty, oozing rot and ugliness.

Late at night, voices began to reach me from a distance, as if they came out of a deep well. Weeping, singing, and groaning came from afar and crept into my ears. In the morning, I took a piece of chalk and drew on the wall a big door, a window, and above the window a bright sun shoulder to shoulder with the discolored words left behind by those who most likely were escorted to death or other cells.

In the next thousand days, the cell was no longer solitary; indeed, it became a vast plain and a beautiful shore, responding to what I wanted or needed, courteously obliged by chalk and walls.

The Cowardly Wheelchair

THE DEMONSTRATORS were getting closer and closer, their voices reaching the firmament. "A paradise, a paradise, oh, homeland!"

And so boomed the chants. Shivering, I waved from my open window and raised my voice in an attempt to reach them. A mixed shower of rice and flowers fell on their heads, lifting the voices even higher. From Station Street going up to Idol Square, a sudden swarm of bullets attacked the chorus of chanters. Mike—a *nom du guerre* he went by—fell. He was hurriedly carried away by his comrades, his eyes like glazed jewels, his blood flowing in spurts.

Someone—neither from our quarter nor a previous acquaintance—saw me and yelled, "You, coward, hiding behind that window, why don't you be a man and come down with us?" As the crowd was moving away, the blood became a bright red stream. I tried to push the wheelchair—my companion for the past two years—closer to the window. Coward, coward! The red rivulet stretched and stretched.

A Freshman at Za'atari

O N THE FIRST NIGHT, she snuggled up to him like a little girl frightened by a monster in grandma's fairy tales.

Warmth radiated off him like a melodious dirge. She said, "Tell me about love, and don't stop even if I fall asleep." The wind was a restless steed, furiously neighing; the rain drops of the early fall like the harmony of a monotonous military march. He went on about love, her nose buried in his chest, butterflies hovering in her dreams.

The street, the bedroom, Om Waheed's voice, street peddlers, bullets, the roaring helicopter overhead. *Who are you, you worthless nobody? I will blow you up to the seventh heaven so that not even the blue flies will find you!* The tent in the Za'atari Refugee Camp still stood firm in the face of the storm, and she continued looking for warmth on his chest.

The Man with Glasses

His dark glasses became a part of him. I haven't seen him without them for years. He used to say, "These glasses are the only thing that doesn't recognize that the earth revolves around itself."

His height makes him stand out among the crowd. His distinct cologne is a head-turner, so to speak. A human mass was entering Post Avenue leading to Old Clock-tower Square. He was at the center of this mass, directing it with his hands to come forward. Chants rose to a pitch, with him in the lead shouting, "To freedom! We march forward, to freedom!"

A roaring car approached. Only one voice rattled on, his voice . . . sticky silence. Time seemed viscous, standing still. Footsteps approached. His feet were rooted in the asphalt like an electric pole. I was hiding like a rat. I heard someone tell him, "Run like the others! Run or I will kill you!" He was the only demonstrator in the square where the clock had been pointing to ten for years.

The fully armed policeman drew closer and gruffly lifted off his glasses, only to put them back jerkily in place, surprised to see his spent eyes. He headed towards a narrow alley, apparently disgruntled. I thought I saw something glistening running down his cheeks.

Acculturation

E VERY EVENING her hair cascaded over his face like a sheaf of wheat. The snows of Scotland and the sun of the East: a kaleidoscope of harmony and disharmony.

He met Kathy—as she wanted him to call her—in Rusholme, Manchester. She would hang on his neck and say, "Tell me about the secrets of Eastern love." And he would say,

"I will tell you about a country that eats its own children and about the grindstone of life on the Euphrates—on one condition."

"What's your condition?"

"I call you Kawthar."

"And I will call you Allen."

Since then Kawthar McDonald and Allen Haj Husain began walking the streets of Manchester, their bodies so close, her hair cascading like sheaves of wheat, he speaking incessantly about the secrets of Eastern romance.

A Habit

BECAUSE THE MILITARY AIRPORT was close to Hannoundi's home, training planes often crisscrossed the air overhead.

Every time a plane was up, Hannoudi—or Muhannad per official school records—would tear off a page from his notebook and run up to the roof so that he, too, would make a plane with which to outrace the acrobatic pilot skillfully dancing with his military plane. It was a habit no amount of warning managed to discourage.

While Hannoudi was practicing his hobby one Friday morning, the pilot relished strafing the town's houses. After the second barrel had landed, Hannoundi's paper kite was gently drifting down the tops of palm trees in the street trying to land, while Hannoudi himself was going up in the air. He must have been trying to look that rat of a pilot hiding in his cockpit right in the eyes.

The next day, the schoolteacher wrote, "Absent, forever" next to Muhannad Al-Hassan's name.

*I won't be disclosing a secret if I say I can't enjoy the
snow, despite its whiteness and purity.*

News Bulletin

Aunt Om Kurayyem had no boys. She was both father and mother after her husband died in the October war against the enemy in the Golan front.

She hung his medals next to his picture, sporting his thick mustache and a high fore-head. The street was besieged, it was heavily pelting bullets.

Om Kurayyem put her two daughters behind her in the corner of the room. His smell was disgusting. He ogled her silent eyes, while the others were searching the house. The evening news bulletins glorified the heroes who chased away the terrorists, but omitted Om Kurayyem's gasps and the blood that seeped through the quarter.

Every morning people saw two wild flowers opening and climbing the city windows, and, when wafted by a gust of wind, they emitted something like a lament.

Orders

"I AM A PALM TREE that grows only in that land, and a river that does not leave its course."

These were the last words Husain said to his friends in the university dorm in Belgrade when he completed his medical studies. He added jokingly, "I can't imagine myself making a living from treating the foul odors in the mouths of my patients."

I saw him later in a military uniform, like a poplar tree along the Euphrates, gathering on his shoulders stars from on high. He had his eyes set on the border. The military car crossed the road and headed north to the border. He had orders to start shelling, the target being that village sleeping in the lap of the olive grove.

A soldier returned from recon and said he had seen in the village a military badge sinking in a quagmire, while the shadow of a tall man left the road and went into a house on whose wall his picture was swinging.

The strange thing was that the village dogs did not bark. Perhaps they knew him.

Lampedusa

THE SKY IS DOWNCAST THIS EVENING, the sea furious, the pirates in a nasty mood, yelling with no evident reason. The dilapidated boat is squeaking, rising and falling.

He scooped some water and slapped the old captain in the blue shirt and ordered him to return the captured water back to the sea. Mumbles and dubious silence.

In the garden of Aleppo University, she was relishing her cup of coffee. I was looking for a proper way to say, "Hello." He reminisces.

T"o remove the Leader's picture from your office is both a conspiracy and a crime." That's all he recalls from the interrogation in the Intelligence Branch.

She would float a little, then disappear. Her lips were bluish, with something like salt on them. She mumbled, "Get away. I don't want you to die. I love you." She was submerged by water. His attempts to rescue her were foiled by her braids. She would float again.

The next morning, Giusi Nicolini, the mayor of Lampedusa, stood before a little grave, saying a prayer. While Omran was feeling his little Quran, the Pope, inserting a little cross as a tombstone for her grave, said, "They run away from war in search of freedom only to find death."

Italy officially mourned the dead, while the Syrian TV aired the Egyptian comedy "Rowdy Schoolboys" for the umpteenth time.

Gawa

"THE SKIES OF MY COUNTRY rain legends. There are as many tales as there are handfuls of sand, and under every tree trunk there lies a buried story whose heroes are you and me in our thousandth version, or five thousandth, no matter," Jalal said to his supervisor, Dr Hayder, in his office at Damascus University, by way of introducing his MA thesis proposal.

When the evils of the Assyrian King Zahhak went beyond all measure, he was cursed, his neck constricted by serpents, his pain alleviated only when life was squeezed out of a human sacrifice. Gawa, the Kurdish blacksmith, managed to rid the world of him.

With a long beard and wandering eyes, Jalal was pacing the narrow corridor in front of his cell. The questions of the interrogator were still ringing in his ears, "Who is Gawa? Who is Zahhak? And what's the story of the land whose skies rain legends and tales?"

While the newscaster announced a cabinet reshuffle, flowers were filling the office of Dr Hayder, the new minister of higher education.

The Ring

CEASELESS, immense energy. She was dressing wounds, carrying the injured, giving a few drops of water to the thirsty—all amid the stench of blood and death, stifled groans, and the endless chatter of wireless devices.

The eyes of Suad, a retired teacher turned nurse in a field hospital, exuded determination and transparent sadness. One day there was so much coming and going. Four-wheel drives roared, and Suad rushed to help. She carried the first wounded, then the second, then the third. When she laid the latter out on the bed, his hand fell quickly on her chest. She gasped. She saw the wedding ring she had bought a month ago with her pension. It was Abdul-Rahman!

The following day she brought his picture, her only son, to the field hospital. With no one to console her anymore at home, she no longer slept there.

The Poet

ON EVENINGS HE turns into a chimp jumping here and there before His Excellency and His guests. He has a steel memory and a bourgeois genteelness.

He can recite from memory the poems of Al-Mutanabbi, the Rajaz poems of Al-Ajjaj and his son Ru'ba, the history of Abu Ja'far Al-Mansour, Al-Mamoun, and Rommel. Sometimes he would sing in a sorrowful tone, or mimic that bald fat actor. Late at night he would enter his room, exhausted, and count his books on their shelves.

He recalls her telling him in their last meeting in front of the college library, "When you go back home tomorrow, your country will celebrate the return of a remarkable academic."

There was another voice—actually voices—piercing the silence. The pillow hugs a head inhabited by a carpentry workshop, seeking a proper opening for a new panegyric befitting His Excellency. Though still a trained, domesticated chimp, he was a master of mourning, verse, and perhaps even caterwauling.

East/West

I WON'T BE DISCLOSING A SECRET if I say I can't enjoy the snow, despite its whiteness and purity, and despite that delicious numbness that permeates embracing bodies on snowy nights, boosting the value of warmth for the weary hearted.

But through the small window of my room on 104 East, Edinburgh, Scotland, I simply watched it fall. My desert memories kept pouring sand on my head, sometimes blurring my vision, while reading the poetry of Imru'l Qays and AL-Nabigha Al-Thubiani. Under my pillow were discolored yellowish papers of a history stained with blood and bile. That tall man with sharp features, presumably the mayor, was overseeing the work as the road was being opened for passersby.

The apologetic poem whose rites I was still living said we were fine, and its author insisted on kissing the ground under the feet of the wielder of the pen, and of the sword.

An Agonizing Joy

IN THE MORGUE OF THE WAR—an apocalypse raging in this forgotten corner of the world—Haj Abdul-Kareem was gathering shreds he was told belonged to his undergraduate son who is, or *was,* getting ready to marry.

At the same time, the joyless widow Om Sa'do was looking for Sa'do—once her only survivor of the vicissitudes of fortune. She found the shreds of a leg torn by a bomb, but Haj Abdul-Kareem insisted they belonged to his son. She screamed in his face, "I'm a woman worth a thousand men, and you won't take a shred of my son's body."

The armed overseers of the morgue intervened. So she offered them the evidence: the scar from the surgery in his knee after a bad fall in a football game. She was triumphant; she carried the leg, overjoyed. Then she and the bereaved father both burst into tears. Her triumph was like defeat, agonizing joy.

Constitution

THE PAVEMENT chanted for them, and the asphalt kissed the ground under their feet. The traffic light had only one color—green, the color of the homeland.

Bricks were grouchy this morning, and fog conferred its own awe on things; ambiguity calls for fear and apprehension. People were crossing the subway tunnels without reading the morning papers; strangers nursing their solitude—that's exile.

The newscaster did not desist from glorifying the victories of our 'eagles.' Achieved, of course, against women and children.

Embrace

E VERY MORNING passersby crane their necks when they cross the city square. His body is still warm, and in its bent position there is something soft like a tune.

She lets her coal-black braids down on his chest, and pouts as if about to divulge a buried secret. I close my eyes out of shyness. Thirty years per the tally of figures.

As he is wont to do, every morning he protects her from the storm, and she tells him her secrets. The city is violated by foreign bodies. The marble of the two lovers still cold and warm in the middle of the square, their eternal embrace unnoticed by the hurried passersby.

III

*Sophie or Sophia—she had too many names—would hang
around his neck and whisper, "Why don't you just forget about
this East of yours, its superstitions and heaps of vintage sorrow?"*

A Role Model

AND THE CLOUDS were crossing, a memory already laden with them, the heart, like an autopsy room, was packed with dismembered limbs.

In the 1973 October war I was not shot. I shot myself in the feet, and was given a hero's welcome in the hospital. In school I never made it to the top rank. I was a total dunce in math and history. I offered small bribes to get some recognition, and I received too many slaps from the rowdy elements in the school, and I never once fought back.

Today when I came home late, it was not because my boss had invited me for a cup of coffee; no, he spat in my direction. And I was wise enough not to respond, but simply smiled obsequiously!

My son Adnan was resting his little head on his hands while doing a homework assignment. I surreptitiously looked over the title, "My Father Is My Role Model."

The Cripple

To WALK WITH YOUR head high amid crowds gathered in front of a football stadium or theater, to race with others from the beginning to the end of the pathway in Lovers Garden, to go up the stairs to your room on the top floor without hanging on the railings, to look that woman straight in the eye and prepare to say "I love you" without having to tremble—these are the impossible desires I belatedly discovered.

Since my release from the detention center, the German wheelchair has been accompanying me even in dreams. And "cripple" is the latest addition to the roster of my names.

The "German wheelchair" is a device used for interrogation that is said to have been devised by the Stasi and supplied by East Germany.

On Love and War

SHE WAS WIPING THE DUST off time's mirrors, and synchronizing her heart's clock to the ticking of his eyes when she said, "Why do men become gentler during wars so that their desires sprout like little flowers in the Syrian desert after rainfall?

Why does the child in them burst into screaming and trifling so that their souls are poured like the scent of rosewater in a Damascene coffee cup?"

He said to her, "In war, endings get closer and closer, and the gap between desire and silence narrower. That's why I am afraid to die without telling you about my dream last night!"

Oh, I forgot to tell you that the bullet snapped up the rest of the tale; none knows their secret save the sniper on top of the opposite building.

The Memoir

I ABSOLUTELY STILL THINK the Euphrates is not a river like, say, the Seine or the Danube because I once heard it singing for lovers, and with my own eyes saw it weeping when our neighbor drowned in it one cold stormy evening as she was trying to bring water for her animals.

I also heard it crying for help when a pilot attacked it with a sudden rocket, and a deep sigh—thought it was an Iraqi song that came out of the breast of its waters! I saw something like a blood fountain towering over a Euphrates willow in the middle of one of its islets. I told it a secret—which I cannot tell you—and it laughed a lot.

I told some immigrants to carry with them a little of its water—they might need it when they drown off the shores of Greece or Malta. "Just mix it with seawater and then drink to your heart's desire."

Found in the memoirs of Drowned Body No. 1963, handed to me by Greek border police, dated 8 March.

Forged

CRETAN COAST GUARDS celebrated Thanksgiving aboard their boat while cruising up and down the coast; that's all they could afford on this cold night.

They wished they were with their families, but duty is duty. Luminous objects floated on the surface; the boat approached—they were drowned bodies unserved by life vests soaked in water and woe, flung up and down by the arms of mountain-like waves.

A woman, fighting death, was still holding her crying baby in hopes he would live. A passport was also sinking, not far off. Dimos the soldier cautiously reached out to pick up the passport and very politely handed it over to his commander who opened the first page, bottom-upped his glass, and mumbled, "Forged!" The Thanksgiving party went on, luminous objects were still seen, but they began dimming.

Fire

WE ARE SO STUCK to certain habits that they become permanent and distinct, like fingerprints.

Among these are crossing the old Raqqa bridge at night, wandering in the eastern market in morning, drinking coffee after dawn prayers with Uncle Tawfeek, collecting the red rose from the small window of the kitchen that separates us from the neighbors, reading the verses of vagabond poets and Amal Dunqul. That's quite an irony I have often asked myself about without an answer!

In detention you rearrange yourself in order to discover the precise order; and then you laugh at it with what's left of yourself; guards rush to you and whip your bare back—perhaps their senses have detected the fire of your memory.

Black Holes

IN THE PHYSICS AUDITORIUM, Professor Imran exerted himself explaining black holes in distant galaxies; at the same time his heart was counting those of his own.

When he was a student at Cambridge, he was like a hummingbird chasing after flowers in the college gardens or like the bank of the Cam. Sophie or Sophia—she had too many names—would hang around his neck and whisper, "Why don't you just forget about this East of yours, its superstitions and heaps of vintage sorrow?"

He would laugh like a child and, mocking seriousness, explain, "The East is a vital sphere; whoever falls into it will forever rotate like a satellite in an unchanging orbit." In the Interrogator's Bureau, opposite Al-Jahiz Garden in Damascus, he jotted down the names of all those he had met at the university and the dorm, during travels and trips.

The interrogator shook his head and scribbled, "To be transferred to Dorm 4." Later on, he came to believe it was reserved for those with black holes in their hearts.

Cabal

"PEOPLE AGREE on codes and meanings; hence language." Remember? Wasn't this what Fayez Daya, professor of linguistics, had said?

You were then wearing a gray winter coat with a fur collar. And from that day on, you and I agreed to make our own language.

I am not eager to see you means *I'm dying to see you. I don't care about what you say* means *I was waiting on pins and needles. I won't come back to this place means I won't budge. I have not known another woman before you* means *none of them left any trace in my memory!*

I wanted to tell you about this alphabet of ours before you boarded that damned boat. I think it would have spared you the trouble of learning another language. I tried to scream, but my voice could not cross the sea.

The Good Afternoon Rose

THE RELATIONSHIP between man and things remains a mystery. For instance, I could never understand the relationship between my friend and his dog Sasha.

It was neither friendship nor sympathy nor love. The same goes for my relationship with a climbing plant I was once given. I planted it in the corner of the garden and it crept on the wall of my room. Because I am a nocturnal creature who sleeps during most of the day hours, its roses used to open at exactly the moment I woke up. Its leaves spread whenever I touched them lovingly; it preserved the dew for me and filled the place with its aromatic fragrance. That good afternoon rose—as it was called—used to wait for me like a lover, and I would hug it like a child.

I forgot to mention that the same rocket that scooped out my eye uprooted it too. But it stuck to the wall despite its burned leaves. I still see it every day—with one eye. But I can't understand why this good afternoon rose continues to wait for me.

Government

IN MY MINI GOVERNMENT, I was the rebellious rogue who always resisted repression, mother being the populace whose ethos was "to hear is to obey," and my brothers the rabble.

Only little Amjad was an opportunist who always got what he wanted, though in his own way. At one time, he is the sick one who needed care; at another the gifted one who needed support; or yet again the much awaited traveler. My father represented absolute authority and the upper hand that doled munificence.

On the stage of that beautiful house we were actors who excelled in playing out their parts delightfully. That was what I wanted to tell you, but the booming explosions in the near train station bespeak a massive coup d'état. I think it will sweep my mini government, too.

IV

Rain was battering the skin of the tent like
the claws of a bird of prey.

The Rifle

M Y FATHER was a skillful hunter, but he could not bring me to appreciate his hobby.

While he considered this an act of ingratitude on my part and a failure in my upbringing, he always respected my wishes. He would not enter my room in his hunting gear, and would often hide the blood of his game from me, and he would not invite me to eat of his kills. He knew I was a vegetarian.

These are things I tell to my colleagues at the checkpoint, with my finger ever on the trigger, what with blood being the constant rain, the university a thing of the past, and the big certificate still hung on the wall of my memory.

"Father," I said, holding his tombstone, "I am no longer what I was; now you would be able to enter my room with your string of headless sand grouses, bleeding from under your leather belt. Blood is really nothing more than a red liquid."

London Eye

I HAD OFTEN PRACTICED my hobby riding those Ferris wheels—like gigantic fans—on the Thames.

When they flung me up in the air, I felt an ecstasy I could not then fathom. Perhaps they gave me a sense of control or superiority over others because I saw them as very, very small. Even Parliament House and the royal palaces looked small. It is a unique feeling to be on top.

Perhaps I now for different reasons wish there was Damascus Eye, Aleppo Eye, etc. Perhaps I want to try feeling what it is to be higher than your jail, to see my jailer as an invisible despicable being, and the informer's car as a black blip—really more like a boil than anything else—on the skin of the road.

Only tree tops are near you, with birds beating their wings over the distant horizon.

A Ritual

ABU HUSAIN is a yeoman worker who has daily rituals which he holds as almost sacred: he prays the dawn prayers in the neighborhood's mosque; he is infatuated with the incantation of Sheikh Mahmoud whenever he recites, "And when a baby-girl buried alive is asked for what sin she had been slain."

He makes his own black coffee, goes to the bakery and buys 2 loaves, lingers a little in front of Al-Jazeera restaurant to inhale the odors of roasted meats, then moves on to Holy Mecca Sweets and buys nothing. He caps his rituals by buying a small can of beans.

He still adheres to the same rituals despite the four years of war, though with a slight modification: Shaikh Mahmoud died of torture; the bakery, the restaurant, and the sweets shop were all blown to smithereens. Nevertheless, he says, "I still smell the odor of bread, roasts, and *kunafa*. I have such a sense of smell I think 1 my seventh ancestor was a dog."

He then succumbs to a sob-like laughter, but this time the can of beans he has is courtesy of the Relief Commission.

Death Dance

THOSE WHO ESCAPE from the hell of the times carry a detailed history of their lives. They run towards the distant horizon, ecstatic with disappointment, their eyes being like guillotines for unconsummated dreams.

They vacillate between a sky that has not let water through its sheath for too long and the parched earth beneath it. The mother told her children, "You can choose only one thing to carry with you. I don't think we will ever come back to this country that rains death." Abboud carried his kitten, Furat, the teenager, took his guitar, while she herself carried a photo showing her in a white bridal dress, lovingly hugged by a man.

She said, "I think the death dance has begun and, in this purgatory of life and war, we are only heading on the path towards it."

Silent Clamor

PILES OF HUMAN FLESH were sardined in a transnational express train in that country.

They were immigrants to a dream that might turn out to be a nightmare. This gentle blonde chap might be from Aleppo; and that dark one with harsh features might be from Raqqa or Dera'a; while that peaceful woman with sad eyes, looking like she is in love, could be either from Homs or Hama.

"Do you have children who play with you or ride your back like a donkey? Do you enjoy being a donkey as I do sometimes?"

"How do you pro-rate your wages at the end of the day? By the head or some other way

"Did you dance in weddings?"

These were questions I did not dare to put to soldiers who manned the checkpoints on the road to Hatay and checked my ID. When I left the border I wished I had. But the silent clamor was more worthy of my voice—what with the snipers monitoring the squinting in my eyes or the pouting of my mouth.

Waste Partners

THANKS TO THE OFFICES of good Samaritans, our warlord and theirs agreed to a ceasefire provided that everything is equally divided. Thus we assembled the dismembered limbs under an ancient walnut whose trunk was cracked and deeply furrowed by the passage of time.

"This head is ours, and that is yours. These ten fingers are ours, and you take the same number—the same goes for feet, eyes, and ribs. This destroyed street is yours, the one after it ours. The burned trees in that bush are ours, and yours those in the next one."

As bullets pierced the skin of the clouds in celebration of this division of waste, each one of us took his share and drove burning wedges in the ground to mark his borders and to warn trespassers.

We put up a sign in all languages that said, "These are the borders of our kingdom whose citizens are the transient and the dead."

Garbage Collector

THE STREET is almost empty of its wealthy people who carried their treasures and left.

Dr Adnan is now in Sweden, Ali the engineer is in Denmark, and Comrade Nidhal defected and took his share of the homeland to Istanbul. This was what old Abu Ahmad mused to himself as he stopped in front of the gates of beautiful villas for a minute or more. For years he's been in charge of cleaning the streets in Palaces Quarter and monitoring the changing fates of its residents, as if he were a tax collector. However, he could not hold his tongue regarding the fate of Abu Hayder.

"This bastard," he whispered, "stayed behind to trade in everything. He has already bought half of the houses in the quarter at a quarter of their price." Then he screamed, "I can clean the filth in your streets, but who can clean your other filth? Only we the poor stayed behind in the homeland; perhaps one day you will come back as freedom fighters and leaders."

He continued to sweep the street, this time without wages or perks.

A Marvel

MANY ARE THE THINGS Sheikh Tayseer claims for himself. Even the title of *sheikh,* it is he who gave it to himself.

During the war he showed total indifference to what was going on around him. He kept telling people about marvels happening to him and how bullets would not harm him. When rockets fell, he would come out unscathed, often laughing, and deliberately raising his hands up in nervous motions. But the most important marvel he claimed was that whatever *surah* or verse he recited, its promise would be unfailingly fulfilled.

On his way back home from a recent trip to Damascus—there he had seen another life where young boys and girls were having fun, rich people cruising the streets in luxury cars, and warplanes flying overhead carrying explosive barrels and heading north—he recited aloud, "And then we sealed their ears in the den for a number of years." But in secret he would continue, "You would have seen the sun, when it rose, veering away from their den towards the right and, when it set, moving away from them to the left."

As if stung, Sheikh Tayseer jumped and said, "And their dog stretched its forelegs in the threshold." He kept repeating these last words incessantly.

Confessions

I TOLD YOU THE LAST TIME we had met over the new bridge that I did not fear death, that I had a brave heart, that I would defend my convictions like a man.

On that day, I watched the sparkle in your eyes, and to tell the truth I liked it very much, and I felt that the military uniform complemented the scene and conferred dignity upon me.

Now we are besieged. I have only a few bullets in my magazine, and I feel the air is too heavy and the surrounding mountains are closing in upon us. Some numbness is creeping up my legs. That's why I decided to confess to you that I am *not* what I said I was. At school, I was a coward. I was the first to take to his heels in fights between our neighborhood and our neighboring Workers Quarter. I had often suffered from nocturnal incontinence whenever I was bullied by Abdo the Bear . . .

One of those around him said later, "He had so much more he wanted to say before he fell silent."

The Poem

HE WAS SUCH A POET as to make bread out of words, to imbue them with the titillating scent of *tannour,* and sprinkle his letters with rosewater.

He attunes his verses according to the rhythms of his heart, thus making his ideas pliable to his wishes. He scatters their brilliance over the braids of his beloved every morning, and sings for the earth, people, and sand grouses at harvest time.

Today in his tent near the Turkish border all he can do is try to hold it when the storm picks up momentum. Rain was battering the skin of the tent like the claws of a bird of prey. What's left of his language is bread and *tannour;* rosewater and brilliance were gone; sand grouses changed their path to a safer course.

"We are waiting for your singing," she said.

"It is the only thing that does not need permission from anyone."

"I'll try."

Their neighbor asserts that he heard something like sobbing.

V

He whispered to her, "No cucumbers smell like Aleppo cucumbers, no tomatoes taste like Raqqa tomatoes, not to mention Idlib olives."

A Brush Dipped in Earth

PROFESSOR GIULIANO of the Arts Academy of Rome told him once that his brush was dipped in the earth of his little town sleeping on the bank of the Euphrates.

On that day he laughed with ecstasy and said, "The Euphrates, Professor, is one of the rivers of paradise. That's why the color of its clay appears in all my paintings. But I, unlike you, can smell the earth in them as well." The professor then gave his usual guffaw, and his pipe nearly dropped from his thin lips.

Now the artist went back to that same place in the World Exhibition of Modern Arts from which he has been absent for years, and his former professor said to him, "Your colors are no longer what I have known them to be. They are more like something burning, stained with blood and death. There is nothing in them that is reminiscent of life."

He gave a withered smile and said, "But, Professor, my brush still gets dipped in the earth of my town! Only this time, you all can smell it, if you wish."

The Jackass Journalist

HE WENT INTO THE OFFICE of the editor-in-chief and left the door ajar. He offered him a file containing a few papers, then retreated a little.

The phone kept ringing, the pictures of the Leader, smiling mysteriously, and his family were hung on the wall behind him. The tall-poled flag nearly blocked the sun rays from his frowning face. He said, "So, you put the blame on the leadership and absolve the traitors, the saboteurs, and the riot-mongers!"

Until this moment, his file is his only pillow, accompanied only by humidity and darkness in that corner of a forgotten world. Remembering that he still belonged to the 'Fourth Power,' he decided to skip number 4 whenever he counted down: 5, 3, 2, 1. Now he hears the guard calling the jackass who was once a journalist.

Infatuation

E VERY MORNING SHE picks red and white roses from the garden.

She takes advantage of his absence in the clinic to clean the petals well, listen to Mozart in between intervals of listening to Fairuz, enter the bedroom with matchless passion, arrange the red petals in the form of a heart whose center she strews with white ones. That's all that's left for her after graduating from the College of Fine Arts. The fragrance wafts up and scales the walls to the neighbors, drawing knowing smiles on women's faces behind those walls.

She did this every day, but the bed remained empty, cold, silent. She swore she would never deprive it of her rose formations, for the Doc—as he was called by the neighbors—was still detained by his ruthless captors on charges of "weakening the national spirit by treating wounded demonstrators."

She went on listening to Mozart, every morning holding her basket of roses on her arm.

That Country

BECAUSE SHE knew he was a vegetarian, she ordered him lots of salads and special foods for "eccentrics"as she insisted on calling them.

He preferred the French-style little restaurant at the end of Moulin Rouge for its coziness. He simply looked at the food, while she was gulping down hers with excessive relish. He drank lots and lots of water; the dryness in his throat bespoke a looming disaster.

He whispered to her, "No cucumbers smell like Aleppo cucumbers, no tomatoes taste like Raqqa tomatoes, not to mention Idlib olives." Sticky silence reigned supreme. Paris disappeared completely from his sight. A volcano was about to erupt, while Fleura declaimed on her fondness of French cuisine.

As for the restaurant manager, well, he promised to reconsider his menu.

The Task

To see the Euphrates as a bluish, greenish thread from his cockpit was all too familiar to him.

He has spent several years in the Tabqa Military Airstrip, and in the meantime loved the delicacy of *thareed,* a mutton and wheat bread porridge, the locals offered to their guests. This time, his task was to bombard terrorist positions in the nearby city of Raqqa. He circled over the Old Bridge and then swooped down on the target by the National Hospital. A cloud of smoke and fire rose up, a mass of groaning formed, and eyes were frozen by horror.

While he was listening to the accolades of his commander for his "precise targeting" and receiving his reward, some radio station announced that twenty young students from the High School of Commerce were missing. He was still counting the bank notes—stamped with the Leader's picture—when his wife urged him to buy sweets for the droves of guests who would come in the evening to congratulate him.

The Delusion Monger

A T SCHOOL, most of our sandwiches somehow landed in his belly.

The teacher once said to him, "You, chimp, can sell even delusions to others and receive payment for them as well." This chimp has in fact convinced us that he could offer us many services: he could have this one enlisted in the football team, and that one appointed class leader, another one awarded a certificate of appreciation. Indeed, he could do many things because he exploited the dubious relationship between his mother and the school principal. This was some thirty years ago.

Amid the raging war now, he is trusted by everyone. He can sell fuel, clothes, property, passports, and security approvals to renew passports; he prays in congregations and perfumes the hands of worshipers at the mosque's gate as well.

The Unsayable

WHEN THE STREET is emptied of pedestrians, the asphalt rent its face in mourning over them, sparrows abandoned their flight, walls whispered to one another unspoken secrets that once were locked in infatuated hearts now carrying their tales and traveling lightly to a country that neither sang nor lamented like them.

They looked for cities that were like them, cities that had the scent of anemones, *achillea,* and wormwood. He whispered to her, "Cover me with your braids, for the eyes of these pierce my voice and leave me dumb."

She buried her head in his chest and said, "That's all we've got left of our homeland that drained water from our eyes; and here we are nursing our woes all alone." The asphalt is sunken of cheek in sorrow, the sparrows have abandoned flight, and she insists on burying her head in his chest and saying the unsayable.

This is what a certain writer left behind; perhaps it was a tentative novel, a story, footnotes, a scrap of paper found in a burned house.

The Mask

LITTLE ACTORS jumped on the stage like bunnies, trying to mimic their roles. The director took pains to follow the course of their motions.

But he was moving extremely cautiously, often hiding one of his eyes—a burned out pit left by treacherous shrapnel. In drawing class he painted faces with one eye, even his plaything was one eyed. In the school textbooks given to him by the Relief Commission in the Turkish Gaziantep Refugee Camp, he blotted out one eye from the pictures of any child, horse, or sparrow.

On the night of the closing ceremony, the director asked all actors to put on their masks. The striking thing was: they were all one-eyed.

Mulla Sa'doon

"YOUR LEG must be amputated, Sir!" said a French doctor volunteering for Médecins Sans Frontières to Sa'doon, the Holy Idiot or, as women called him, the Blessed Mullah.

"Plant it next to the last olive tree in my father's farm," replied Sa'doon. He insisted he saw a light shining every night from the last row of olive trees in Abu Faris's farm. He pointed with his hand to something that looked like lightening; women laughed and stroked his dangling locks of hair.

"From now on, our task is to shoot down helicopters from the roof of this destroyed house," said Sa'doon's companions. "My eyes are as sharp as those of a hawk, and my hands are very strong on the trigger," said Faris with a sly smile.

Like Stones

IN THE PAST, she would carry your heart with endless pain, scatter words and strip them naked, only to rearrange them like precious stones into a necklace of poems.

She used to say, "Language is deceptive; it does not give us what we want unless it robs us of our inner peace and what's left of our sense of security." She continued to play her game, but in war things change. Now she lists the names of those who went to meet their Lord; she memorizes their names and arranges them alphabetically, or according to their hair color or the names of their darlings.

She tries to give each one of them what elegy he deserves.

VI

The therapist concluded her report with this recommendation, "No further sessions required."

A Moment

Dawn approached and a stinging cold lashed his forehead, giving him intense pleasure. The voice of the muezzin Abu Ibrahim broke the silence, and it was the first time Dr Amer was not bothered by it.

"I've been a neighbor of this mosque for years," he mumbled, "and this is the first time I feel safe. God is almighty. In wars we look for any safe haven at whose threshold we can bury our fears."

Laughing at his childish features, Samar hugged his head with excessive tenderness. While her fingers were combing his little beard, he went on watching the children's beds to make sure they were still asleep and that they were not up to some mischief, of which he was the usual victim.

The Graveyard

ONE OF THE CURIOUS things about war is that the survivors seek refuge with the dead and feel safe at their tombstones.

The graveyard changes into a city bustling with life at night. That's what used I do every day; I would stand before the tombstone of my friend Imran, the poet, and tease him with Amal Dunqul's verse, "Are all heads equal?" Laughing onto sobbing, I then turn to his neighbor Ali, the artist and the fond sculptor of horses, whose mares have bolted far away. A mortar shell landed close by, but they were neither scared nor did they run.

I was the only coward among them, the only one to run in panic. The date palm, conferring loftiness upon them, stood its ground, while their laughter chased me, "You are still a coward, just as you were."

A Coward

THIRTY YEARS AGO, when I first arrived in Riyadh as an expatriate, my coworker Abdul-Aziz, or Sheikh Abdul-Aziz as we nicknamed him, said laughing, "You are Syrian, but you are neither pale of face nor soft of speech!" I told him, "Oh, Sheikh, I am a Bedouin whose ancestors had accompanied conquerors in the army of Iyadh ibn Ghanam from Yemen to Raqqa."

Courage, poetry, exile, corruption, uprooted trees are only vestiges of words still stuck, like leeches, on the wall of my memory. In vain I try to prevent them from sucking my blood. The survivors in my native neighborhood urge me to continue my escape on the other side of the border. The whirring of bullets and the roaring of helicopters fill the universe. I stumble and rise. I don't know why I wanted to tell Abdul-Aziz, and only now, that I would have been prouder of my ancestors had they been more cowardly than they were.

Weather Forecast

HE USED HIS BLUE EYES and blond hair as assets and, as such, earned the nickname Abu George from the teenagers of our neighborhood.

The game appealed to him, and he capped the act with an English hat he wore in summer and winter, and a massive, roaring, screeching motorcycle. He used to sit in the center of the Oasis Café we patronized, then he would fire such a hot barrage of sarcastic abuse against the highest officials in town that he was apt to attract a chorus of other abusers. Silence would reign supreme in the café, the password being "weather forecast."

In the evening, he would deliver his reports to security branches in the city, and the café customers would be less the following day. A customer who still was a patron of the Oasis Café told me that Abu George, or Ahmad Al-Sheikh officially, still delivered his reports to the new masters of security branches. There is nothing new in this except that he is now Sheikh Ahmad of the long blond beard.

Homeless

I ALWAYS DECLARE THAT it is no secret when I say that I am fond of marginal characters. In my teens I fell in love with Nadia, a half-crazy somnambulist, who in one of her fits gave my name to her father.

My eye was swollen for a considerable time thereafter. I befriended Imran the poet who used to send me to bring food from our house in exchange for lessons in the principles of prosody. This habit stuck with me even when I was on the run. My homeless friend Mac took to sitting by the Scottish Monument in central Edinburgh.

By the way, the last time I saw him he was escaping from the municipal car collecting the homeless on a snowy, stormy night. He simply snatched a bowl of hot soup. In fact I envied him; I wished I were like him. This way I would have spared myself not only a lot of sorrow over a home that was destroyed by soldiers but also the tragedy of losing my friends and family in a land that was my homeland.

On the Shrink's Couch

THE PARAMEDIC put down two men's bags: the first one contained plenty of books, children's photos, and some medicine; in the other there was a bundle of dollars, gold chains, and the head of a statue with a disfigured face. On a slip of paper he scribbled, "These belongings are the property of two Syrian refugees found unconscious following a road accident on Euro Road 406, near the suburbs of Stockholm."

Later on the Swedish psychotherapist tried to revive their memories. She gave each of them a small notebook to draw his own hometown. The owner of books drew a bridge spanning over a big river, children's faces, a date palm, a woman wearing a black silk *abaya,* a burned house; the owner of the statue drew a heavily medaled officer, a palace with a seafront and a red-brick roof squatting on a mountain top, a bottle of wine, a female dancer, and a warplane dropping explosive barrels.

The therapist concluded her report with this recommendation, "No further sessions required."

Shadows

"AFTER THREE GIRLS in a row," said Ali, the Syrian refugee, as he took a picture out of his wallet, "I was blessed with the birth of my first baby boy, so as a token of thanks I planted this tree that nearly blocks the entrance to the house."

When little Firas knew the story later on, he regarded the tree as his twin. Not surprisingly, he observed a ritual whereby he would stand right next to the tree, watch their shadows, and ecstatically say, "My shadow is taller than yours!"

The war years dragged on, and Firas kept his ritual, but his ecstasy lessened. The tree's shadow stretched, not only covering his own but going beyond it. He started to hide under the tree so that the plane would not see his shadow, as he figured. Ali and Firas are now on the run, with nothing but the picture. The tree's shadow gets taller and taller so as to cover the whole house and make it invisible to the plane that hovers overhead in addition to many vultures.

The Mute

DEMONSTRATORS WERE marching up and down our back street. I could not run, so I simply looked through the window pane. I recognized Hakkoum, or Abdul-Hakeem—who doesn't know him in our neighborhood? He was running like a gazelle. He was gesticulating and waving, and other hands responded in like motions. He suddenly stopped; somebody grabbed him by the neck.

"Tell us, who paid you? Who put you to this? Who do you follow?" But Hakkoum would only smile and draw a line on the ground, with a smaller one and an arrow pointing right towards the Noor Mosque, meaning that he wanted to turn right to attend prayers. "Even you, dumb ass?" said the interrogator, laughing.

The interrogator liked the game, so he gesticulated to signify "Why?" The mute drew two hands raised towards heaven in supplication. The interrogator slapped him, "Even you?"

The Ice-Eating Boy

A CAR CAME TO A screeching halt, and a child whose face was blood-stained was thrown out of its back seat. He was the son of our neighbors, just released after being arrested in an Internet café. A muffled sob.

In the following days, all his mother's attempts to dissuade him from his new habit of eating ice came to grief.

"I know that my tonsils will be inflamed, enlarged, or might even block the air passage," he said to the doctor. "But I don't care." He asked the doctor to come closer. "I'm not crazy," he whispered. "I do this on purpose so that my voice disappears and the policeman won't be able to detect it when I chant with the young demonstrators of our neighborhood tomorrow."

The doctor kept the secret until now—even after offering his condolences when there was a lull in the bombardment.

Drenching

SYRIA ABDALLA was found semi-naked in a dark alley. Someone carried her and delivered her to her mother. Sticky silence bordering on squalls ensued.

She insisted on sleeping in the house yard, leaving the door open, and would scream if any door was shut behind her. She would absolutely refuse to take off her clothes, putting up a fierce fight. Her mother found cruel faces sketched on the inside wall of the house: one with a thick mustache, one with a chain around the neck, another with a little nose and a long neck.

Curiously, with relish and triumph she would watch the urine trickle from her legs to the pavement. Perhaps she wanted to drench her rapists in filth.

VII

Behind this particular tree, I had my first kiss.

Graduation Project

THE EXHIBITION HALL of the Faculty of Fine Arts at Damascus University featured a student's graduation project: the painting of a man who fixed his chair on top of a very steep hill whose base looked like the long bones in our bodies: a forearm, a leg, a thigh.

Anatomically speaking, everything was perfectly placed. Its rest—I mean the chair's—was made of compact, interlaced skulls whose eye sockets were too large—as if they were opened more than necessary. A crawling body approached the leg of the chair, separated from it by some distance. On the steep slope others were jostling each other, feverishly trying to get to the top chair. Their bodies were taut, their fingers were grappling for a finger-hold.

I forgot to say that the gate was just closed, weapons rattled, the supervising professor and the student HH were both handcuffed in the back seat of a car with shaded windows. On the main gate to the hall, there was a freshly posted note, "Graduation exhibitions canceled this year in solidarity with our brethren under bombardment in Gaza."

The Fatal Mistake

I DON'T LIKE BIG MEETINGS; I tear up all my little scrap notes; I lower the curtains oftentimes; I leave through the back door of my house. I mostly speak in undertones. I hide half of my face with the collar of my shirt. These are but remnants of my erstwhile clandestine work, which sicken Flora, my British girlfriend.

I hesitated a lot before I answered the questions of the Social Affairs clerk in our neighborhood, east of Manchester. Flora elbowed me, but I ignored her. I feigned idiocy; and in my head I was going over the directives: How to deal with interrogators; don't tell on your comrades; feigned stupidity is your best bet. The whole world turns into a live coal in my hands; life and death are a silly game; beware of the fatal mistake.

Flora alone was patting my shoulder when the clerk's car revved and disappeared behind the bushes.

The Forest

THE FOREST next to our neighborhood was the ideal place to play hide-and-seek after school hours. It was also where we set traps to catch birds. That's how I saw it forty years ago.

Behind this particular tree, I had my first kiss, and in fact, because it had the wonder of surprise and the scent of physical thirst, it remains the most beautiful. This was thirty years ago. It was also in the dead center of that forest that I wrote my first poem, twenty years ago.

The missile that destroyed our mosque also came through that thicket in which the sniper is still hiding, and entertaining himself by killing anything that moves, including our cat whose soft neck was adorned by a collar of blue beads and whose eyes are still open, making my child believe she is playing with him.

The Road to Heaven

THERE ARE NO TRAFFIC LIGHTS on the road to heaven, nor does it have official working hours; it is neither guarded by human beings nor franchised to agents. On it you choose the path that suits your own speed; on it you weep in private and there is someone to hear your sobbing; but there was another murmur I could not make out: Abdul-Hafez was delirious in the detention center set up by the group that took over the neighborhood.

"Prayers, Gentlemen!" The final word was spoken with unmistakable sarcasm through a small window in the iron door by a sparsely bearded youth. His tone was more effeminate than masculine.

After prayers, the emir gave a sermon on mercy while the soul of Abdul-Hafez, the lawyer, was departing from his body. The emir finished his sermon in total confidence and a steady voice. He then finished reciting the Quranic verses of his choice.

The Goalkeeper

"L ISTEN, ABD," SAID the coach of an ancient club. "In a football game, the goal is the team's honor. And when you are the goalie, you must defend it. Don't forget that, Abd!"

On the bus to Aleppo or Hama, Abd, known for his lovely voice, used to sing for the team. He stuck to the habit even in demonstrations, especially the one that started from the old clock tower and marched towards the police headquarters.

"I'm still defending the team's honor, and it is for them that I offer my blood," said Abd, stretched on the floor of the field hospital in the alley next to Sidi Khalid Mosque. This was reported by Fatima, now a nurse, whom we used to call Julie because of her blond hair. I won't be snitching if I say she admired him intensely, I mean, when he was a goalkeeper.

The Wise Doctor

WHEN I HAD BOUGHT HIM a car while he was still an undergrad in the college of medicine, I told him he could give his girlfriend a lift and invite her to lunch just once a month, and he read me the Hippocratic oath whenever I visited him in Aleppo. He asked me cynically, "Am I supposed to preserve the environment by not driving it?"

The fact was he followed my script, with some modifications. For instance, in the demonstrations in the Saladin Quarter, he would walk behind the masses to pick up the wounded and treat them in his apartment. Mehriz Isber, a plainclothes soldier assigned to infiltrate the demonstration, was his guest tonight.

"You must keep silent; I am bound by the oath to treat you. I won't ask you about your job, the city of your birth, or religion. After all, this is the condition by which I can keep the car." Mehriz did not understand a thing. He tried to open his mouth while the doctor was stitching his wound. The wound continued to bleed, but a bit less.

A Two-Storied Country

SOOTHING AND DISTINCTIVE, THE VOICE of the muezzin in that mosque did not reach him clearly except at dawn. What made him certain of the approaching sunrise was the addendum to the *azan*, "Prayer is better than sleep." This is how things went in his cell, forty steps exactly, under the ground.

In the same place among the trees of the park in front of the ancient café, he heard the very voice of the muezzin. The surprise landed on him like a thunderbolt. Horrified, he unbuttoned his shirt and began counting the black scars on his chest, left by cigarettes extinguished with unbridled sadism by his jailer. Laughing, he said to his son who helped him sit, "Blessed art thou, for we have bequeathed unto thee a two-storied country. Choose yours, son!"

There was a teardrop trying to find a place for itself on the map of sorrows felt by Colonel Joseph, a former artillery officer. He mused with a smile, "Perhaps, under the roots of this tree, I have spent ten months."

His case file was closed with these words, "It has been unequivocally proven that the Leader's picture in the colonel's office fell off on account of the poor quality of the homemade thread with which it was strung, and for no other reason."

The Bridegroom

THE STEAM was gathering in the bathroom like a cloud of perfume. The clear sky over that sleepy town in eastern Syria was turning into a beautiful tapestry. His colleagues insisted that he trim his beard; they were screaming their chant, "Joy to our lovely groom!" Their voices intermingled as in a chorus.

Of course, this was before the shell landed; the steam turned red, the singing became a howl of muted sobs.

In every wedding party over the past three years, Hajja Ayesha, mother of architectural engineer Ibrahim, has been seen carrying a small bag that contained a comb, a bottle of perfume, and hair spray. She wants to make sure every bride is ready to meet her groom on their wedding night.

The Flower Man

THREE RED FLOWERS, TRIMMED and dewy, are a lover's gift.

-A bouquet of yellow flowers with no strong scent are for an admonishing or jealous heart.

-White roses say to your partner, "I have forgiven you!"

This was a daily routine for the florist, with a BA in French, setting up shop at the end of our street. Knowing your mood from the glint in your eyes, he chose the right flowers for you. On private evenings, Ghiath, deservedly nicknamed the Flower Man, used to play his guitar with virtuosity.

In the morning, the flowers were withered, crestfallen, scentless, their thorns protruding irregularly. Even the Damascene roses were more like fake ones. Next to them was Ghiath, a coiled body, thrown from an official car that had sped with vigor. Those who saw it can only remember the eagle printed on the rear glass, poised to take flight from the bevy of green stars surrounding it.

The First Dose

Y OU COULD BEAR YOUR SCAR and smile. Your scar is yours, your smile is for others, he mused. Why do doctors lie? Why do we consider their lies an act of courtesy and good conduct?

"Severe weight loss, loss of appetite for whatever food available, and the dull epidermis are all helpful signs in diagnosis," said Dr Ahmad in Gaziantep Hospital. He said, laughing, "To be a refugee is understandable, but to bring along all of your ailments!"

The whole world turns into a surrealist tapestry in which red and black are interwoven, with nondescript shapes this morning. In the hospital's lounge he was, to the surprise of other patients, surrounded by his friends, all with shaved heads.

He was the only one who understood their message. He simply smiled and signed the consent form to take the first dose; Siham, his friend, pointed to her new haircut, somewhat apologetically.

VIII

*He drew a ship in the likeness of a dragon breathing out
smoke and fire and burning every passing cloud overhead.*

A Burned Out Memory

BEFORE THE STORMS and imminent change of weather marking the forty days of dead winter, those with horror-filled hearts gather firewood and dead tree trunks.

"Because I will die before winter, I won't take part in gathering tree trunks," said the grandmother.

"I think I'm marrying in the beginning of the fall, so I can do without more burdens," said Khadija, the beautiful girl whom Ismael had promised to marry.

"I'm getting ready to immigrate and continue my studies abroad. So, why strain myself for others?" said Mamoun, a fresh high school graduate.

When snow and explosive barrels began falling murderously together, the grandmother was still alive, Ismael broke his promise because he had died in the war, Khadija remained single, and Mamoun joined the local team of paramedics. Warmth is an impossible dream, and snow is another murderous tyrant. I have heard this story from my grandmother a thousand times.

The Map

I WAS AN IDIOT in most academic subjects, deservedly earning the epithet "dumbass" in math.

But my ability to draw a map of our country was striking; I made many zigzags in the west bordered by the Mediterranean, drew an ear up north, used a ruler to draw the eastern border, then galloped south in a streamline. I laughed a lot when my map omitted our occupied territories.

Forty years later, I made a thousand failed attempts to draw this selfsame map; apparently the sea was tumultuous, its northern ear was lopped off, and the lines kept changing every morning, artillery erasing the rest, mountains towered taller and blocked the fresh sea breeze off Homs.

Balance

H E USED TO TELL HER, "I have to do an x-ray for you—just to make sure you have a spine and so that I can put my medical specialty in the service of love!" And then she would jump and surprise him with a kiss, sparking fires of nostalgia inside him, and turning his world into a garden of lilies and chrysanthemum. She, tiptoeing like a nimble gazelle on the balance column, often returned home with the championship cup in gymnastics. She did this since she had golden locks until college.

When she told him of her dream to continue her training and studying in the Ukraine, he would mumble, "I know these girlie gambits!" He remembered this as the elevator's door opened and he pushed her wheelchair for her upcoming physiotherapy session. They needed a lot of rest after their escape from Idlib, now ablaze with explosives.

"I admit you have realized my dream," she said to him. "Here we are in the Ukraine. I, too, will realize your x-ray dream—just to prove to you I have a spine, albeit with a bullet lodged next to it."

The Dynamo

H E EARNED THE nickname "Dynamo" from the first coach of the football team in the ancient city club. He was the spearhead that often ended the attack, and was always rewarded with a kiss from his girlfriend who insisted on attending all matches amid a predominantly male audience.

The grass in the play field got burned perhaps for the tenth time and by the same warplane. The odor is implacably planted in his nostrils. The ashes of the goalie's body are still afloat on the small puddle made in the corner of the field by the rain. Dynamo insisted on coming for training on time, despite the sniper, to play in his favorite lineup of 4-4-2.

But this time, he played attack, defense, goal-keeper, referee, and, if necessary, gave himself a red card, while the rest of the team were either detainees, refugees, or martyrs. He still played in the same lineup every day.

Monodrama

H E WAS NOT NINE YET, but his flowing coal-black hair and deep-set eyes gave him extra years. I used to see him every morning, emerging from his tent and carrying his schoolbag on his back.

He would always tell me that he was going to school. He would stop in the courtyard of the camp near the Turkish border and salute a flag that no longer existed. Later on he would get out his food and eat it, saying it is now break time. Then he would sit down and extremely politely apologize for being indifferent to my questions, saying it was class time and he did not wish to upset a teacher who had died under torture.

He would play the hat game by hiding his hat behind him and then exert himself looking for it, and when he found it he was genuinely overjoyed by his discovery and success.

I would walk behind him. He would not stop, just meandering on his own *via dolorosa*, with me following close behind. He neither reached his destination nor did the pain cease. We stopped only at curves to salute a flag that no longer existed.

Cargo

H E COILED UPON HIMSELF on the small economy seat while the airplane was zipping through the skies. On that day, he refused to eat his meal; he simply followed the flight of clouds passing by his round window.

His hand was clutching the only small bag he had brought with him from his homeland. He decided not to come back; he had written poetry and folk songs; his time was sticky and dark and he was addicted to looking up at the skies.

Now he resists surrender. In his waking moments, he defeats his coma in that remote hospital. In the log of unescorted patients he wrote, "Bury me in that piece of land I had bought on the bank of the Euphrates by correspondence. I know this is against my principles, but I still see my homeland not fit for living, but very fitting in death."

The national press said an expatriate poet had returned home on a domestic airline—courtesy of The Leader. But it did not say that this time he came back as cargo.

The Syrian government pays for the return tickets of its own expatriate citizens provided that they be dead.

Two Graves, One Body

As soon as he regained consciousness, he whispered in the ear of his friend and doctor who amputated his left leg, the one smashed by a missile, "Listen Doc, I want a proper grave for my leg here amid the olive trees of Idlib." The doctor laughed, evading tears about to burst like torrential spring downpours.

"We will. And I will also write on the tombstone some lines from your last poem."

"But you don't like my poetry!" he retorted promptly.

"That was before the revolution. Now things are different."

The sky was raining fire, flocks of birds were escaping, and a cloud, shaped like two lovers, hovered over the media center bombarded just a while ago. Ambulances tried in vain to enter the area, and the camera was still on, recording the groans and last words of its owner.

"I want you to bury me here in Raqqa. As I said before, I won't agree to your bringing my buried leg from its grave over there. Out of pure revenge I want to have two graves in my country which did not give me one house; I'm taking two graves . . .

That's all the camera recorded before the paramedics stopped it.

Session 12

1 SHE USED TO VISIT ME EVERY NIGHT, driven by longing. She would sneak into my bed, and when her coal-black hair spread on the pillow, only small spots of gray showed underneath—just like those few sunlit spots left by the thick foliage of an oasis at noon. I am so inundated by her perfume that I swoon for a moment. I crush her and the sky begins to rain perfume.

2 AS NUMBNESS INVADES my entire being, I travel to that city/ town, walk its unpaved alleys barefooted, wipe its window panes in search of some image, and count the stones of the pavement that separates our house from hers. There are forty eight stones, five of them are broken at the corner. There are four sterile palm dates in our neighborhood. That girl is now beautiful, her chest suddenly becomes rounded like two pomegranates from Dar'a.

3 THOUGH I'M A BEDOUIN with a memory like the desert, I often wade in the torrents. That's why the rain always catches me, without an umbrella, by surprise. When the red-haired Dutch therapist with the odd beard read my dreams which I recorded per his instructions, he simply said, "Go now and come back only when your next dream is set over there." And he pointed to the garden next to his clinic.

The Sandwich

SMACKING HER LIPS, she said, "Your food is delicious." He gave up the rest of his sandwich to her, and made do with the cucumber his mother had given him in the morning before coming to school. He whispered to her, "Mother is not good at cooking, but grandma was." Eva, his little Swedish schoolmate, jumped and said, "Bring some of her food next time."

"I can't."

"Does she refuse to give you food?"

He took a picture out of his schoolbag and said, "This is our house in Aleppo, and my grandmother drowned off the shores of Greece. She lied to us, saying she knew how to swim. She left us. That's why I don't want her food." In tears, he tried to put a brave face.

Eva gave him a hug. He asked her to back up his refusal to go on the school trip to the port, saying he hated the sea. She remembered the sketch he created in drawing class in which he drew a ship in the likeness of a dragon breathing out smoke and fire and burning every passing cloud overhead.

Phobia

"PLACES HAVE THEIR OWN PULL on people," he used to say in our private meetings to justify his own enamored attraction to Beirut, especially Hamra.

Without him seeing us, we would whisper that he was running away from himself, from the sympathy, the painful pity, of others after the death of his wife. He would say, "Morning coffee has the aroma of her perfume." And he would always choose the last table on the left in Starbucks.

"Who can forget these two green eyes?" he said to the little boy standing behind the metal barrier as he slipped him a few dollars. The boy ran to his mother, sleeping on the pavement not far off. Then he came back, facing his benefactor, and whispered to him, "You're big, but not a man!"

He was thunderstruck by the whisper of the Syrian boy. He was tongue-tied by the surprise. The boy further said, "That's right, you are not a man. When my father returned from the battlefield and was dying, surrounded by his companions, he said when he saw me crying, 'Men don't cry.' And I saw your tears falling in your cup of coffee!"

Since that day, he would shiver and panic whenever we passed by Hamra or sat in a café.

IX

"Auntie, please alert the doctor that he is being watched by the intelligence," he whispers to the veiled woman who lives on the fourth floor.

Lulu

IN RECENT MONTHS, the interests of Abboudi underwent dramatic changes. He no longer waved his little hands to planes passing over his tired head, though he was the son of a pilot who had passed away under torture.

He no longer opened the fridge to steal ice cream behind the back of his brothers—well, because it has been turned into a container to store cracked wheat. He also stopped reciting the national anthem, which in the past he used to do every morning, even on Fridays. Now he is completely preoccupied with Lulu, his green-eyed cat. He would cover her head during bombardment, soak dry bread in tea for her, and feed her his own share.

"Where is the ID card of your friend so that we can put her on the refugee list?" asked the Turkish officer, teasing him. He produced the ID of his sister who has recently been buried in her school-yard, slipped it in the officer's hand, and laughed wistfully.

"But this is the ID of a girl named Laila?"
"Yes, Sir. But we affectionately call her Lulu!"

The Staff

KHALID, AN INSTRUCTOR OF FRENCH in a wretched high school by the train station in a remote town, whispered to his friend, "Enough of your recklessness and frivolity, man!" This was on a Sunday morning during the flag salutation ceremony. The whisper caught the attention of the school's principal, who winked quizzically. "Nothing, nothing," answered Khalid.

On the way home, Khalid's friend volunteered to explain his theory to Collette who teaches music at the same school, "In fact, you stand in reverence to the staff. It is rather ludicrous that you give it a military salute!" He lit a cigarette and blew its smoke high up through his yellowed teeth and roared in laughter. Rooted to the spot by the stunning discovery, Collette started roaring as well. "Yes, my friend. The flag was shredded two years ago, and we stand in reverence to the staff that carried it!"

"The Boss wants you for a few minutes," said a young man toting a big gun and standing by his official car, all doors open.

In the evening, that same staff was dancing on his feet for the crime of "demoralizing the national spirit!"

Dangerously Insane

"TOTAL BREAKDOWN in mental powers . . . suffers from acute psychosis . . . a schizophrenic personality . . . might be dangerous to those around him . . ." These were snippets from the medical report that forced Khalaf Ahmad, a judge in the city's criminal court, into early retirement.

His Worthiness—as he was referred to in the court—made it his business to visit the local government complex every morning. He would visit its departments in a semi-fixed order: Agriculture, Education, Police Headquarters, and finally Finance.

"This is the biggest land thief in our governorate," he would tell the Director of Agriculture, standing in the door. "Half of our arable land is registered under his wife's name." Everyone laughed.

In the hall of Education Department, "Our young generation is lost, thanks to applauding the Leader and doing time in the Ba'th Vanguards!"

"Our finances and taxes are siphoned off into the belly of this bull!" He means the Director of Finance.

There were grunts and laughter at the end of the corridor when a group of informants plotted to stage a fake arrest. They sat him on a bamboo chair and tied him with an electrical cord. But no sooner had his urine trickled down the corridor and its smell flooded their nostrils than they fled.

His eyes brightened with a feeling akin to triumph.

In Search of a Short Life

COFFEE HAS ITS CHARM AND PULL on him. That's why he didn't wait for his host and publisher to welcome him. He sipped his cup with relish.

"You must be carrying your new novel?" That was the only sentence he heard in a lengthy conversation and a professional introduction.

"You started writing very short stories, my dear?"

"A novel spans a whole life, its characters are long-winded and live a long life no longer possible in war." The publisher shook his head, unconvinced.

"The tent I share with four others in the Za'atari refugee camp is too narrow. My characters are in a hurry, they live their lives to the tune of rock and roll not 'This Is My Night.' Half of them are martyrs, refugees, or warlords." I heard him saying these words while I was walking next to him in silence and picking up the papers he was throwing here and there, trying not to stain them with the mud of pavements.

The sky was still overcast with black clouds over the mountains of Amman while I was walking behind him, kneeling and prostrating like someone performing a mandatory prayer.

Current Affairs

ON A PIECE OF PAPER he often drew a map of a city he used to know by heart. He would spread it over the steering wheel whenever a customer asked him to drive him from one neighborhood to another to remind himself who controls it in order to play the right cassette accordingly: the Quran, Qashsoush, or even Ali Al-Deek sometimes.

Fridays are reserved for Haj Said, the old man, whom he drives to the grand mosque. Thursday evenings he drives Khamees, the one-eyed cellphone trader, to the discos of Abu Qubai and brings him back at dawn, stretched in the back seat of the taxi, cautious of the pungent smell of booze.

Even Om Hassan, the pleasure agent, as the young men dubbed her, began cleaning houses for the Immigrant Sisters in Jihad.

"Oh, for the good old days," she whispered wistfully, "when I was Madame Julie in Jounieh, Beirut, and my waist was like a bamboo stem.

And Other Things

EVERYTHING ABOUT HIM suggested he was a film star: his long hair, his deep eyes, his stimulating scent. That's how women and girls in our neighborhood whispered among themselves every time a peddler pushed his vegetable pushcart in front of him. His shy, whisper-like voice betrayed that he was a novice in the business.

"This is from Knight Gallant," he says as he fishes a letter from the bottom of a vegetable sack and hands it to a short plump girl.

"Auntie, please alert the doctor that he is being watched by the intelligence," he whispers to the veiled woman who lives on the fourth floor.

"Mother, dear, don't go out after sunset. The guys will attack tonight. Stay away from the Statue of the Idol." She comments with a sly smirk on her face, "The Idol with the cape draped from shoulders to ankles?"

The wheels of the upturned pushcart were still running, its load scattered all over, it is no longer possible to tell the difference between his blood and the crushed tomatoes of which he has just filled a bag for the short plump girl.

Codes for
War and Revolution

- We are invited to a wedding in Freedom Hall to-night. We will wait for you.
- Children's paradise is their homes.
- The dance has started, the music is getting louder. Don't be late.
- Abu Hayder is waiting for you in front of the Karnak Hotel in his blue car, surrounded by his sons.
- Today Mr Yaseen is a guest at his aunt's.
- It's cold, the clouds are dark, heavy rains are expected.

While our neighbor, the informer, was busy translating the above coded messages for the officer, newly arrived in the city, and assuring him that a demonstration will start any time in front of Grand Hall, and that Mr Yaseen has been arrested by Branch 279, the roaring chants and ululations rose to the heavens.

The young demonstrators were carrying Muhannad above their heads, his blood gushing forth along the bushes lining the pavement. Haven't we said the dance has started?

Courage

HE WROTE IN HIS testimony, "She is the only one who doesn't hide when the bombardment on our neighborhood intensifies. She stays rooted to her spot, raises her head to heaven, and bullets rain between her hands. We hide our faces behind the window to watch her with awe and envy. She is the date palm standing in the center of our house garden."

While she was snuggling up to him, hiding her face in his chest in search of warmth and safety, he told her, "Our guard is brave, so you can sleep well tonight."

In the morning, government trucks were seen loaded with all the palm trees in the city, their fronds roughly sweeping the asphalt. He and she were on a bus heading north towards the border. He was seen carrying a bag in one hand, a sapling in the other.

Who's the Boss?

WHENEVER THE DOCTOR told him to hurry up and get the operations room ready, he thought, "These doctors are cocky, their hearts full of arrogance!" This was before the war.

He made coffee and made sure no sugar, which he loved, was added to it. He took meat and vegetables to Madame, sterilized the clinic with disinfectants, sometimes washed the car after it had rained, and answered the phone with his typical refrain, "The Boss is busy," even if the doctor was just watching "Good Morning, Arabs" on MBC. This, too, was before the war.

After the war started . . .

His cellphone kept ringing, all eyes were fixed on him while he stitched a wound, ran an operation to extract a piece of shrapnel, gathered body parts, stopped to read Al-Fatiha for the departed, and resumed work. Now *he* is the Doc! Whenever the phone rang and the name of his former Boss, Dr Ayman, appeared on the screen of his cellphone followed by the international code 0034, he stuck out his tongue in wicked gratification and simply asked, "What country code is this, folks?"

On Air

SHE CRIED WHILE READING a news report on the sinking of a refugees' boat at sea.

The warning from the disciplinary committee of the TV channel was prompt and swift. "An anchorman should get their head out of the news; you are a professional. You should not have done it. That is a sin in news casting."

On her way to the studio, she sent some money to her mother and brothers. She felt proud and responsible.

"Be ready for a live broadcast of the next video from the battlefield," came the voice of the producer on her headset.

The camera zoomed in too close. Her eyes froze on the big mole on the victim's left cheek. She tried not to repeat the same journalistic sin while the blood of her brother Abdul-Rahman was spurting as if from a fountain of light.

X

Her body is like a piece of music, which she
controls like a tyrannical ruler.

Replacement

"HE FEELS FOR ME, calms down when I pat him on the neck with my hand, and moves closer to me when my hot tears run down my cheeks," he would explain whenever I asked him about his strong horse on which he had a sort of mobile 'supermarket.' The word 'supermarket,' often on my lips, tickled him.

"Sometimes I imagine that I see a tear locked in his wide eyes. Man's relationship to animals is mysterious. He and I are the breadwinners for my family. That's why I pitched a tent for him in our courtyard, and I even share my blanket with him on frosty nights."

Yesterday he was seen, with the saddle on his own back, carting his dead horse towards the Tal Al-Bay'a cemetery, east of the city.

"I want a proper funeral for him," he sobbed.

The neighbors testified that the rocket had left a huge crater where the tent had been.

The Tattoo

THEY ARE PLUMP AND TOUGH; their bodies taut, their women, in particular, captivating. Their breasts are engaged in an undeclared war, their hips are as wide as a fertile plain.

On his first personal sculpture exhibition, he said, "The human body is a miracle. Whenever I see a mountain, the bodies of its people jump through the rocks to my imagination, and it doesn't bother me if you can't see them."

The Municipality of Oslo was quite busy carrying the items of his first exhibition here. His sculptured figures are emaciated, with sticking bones, and his women hide their faces for some reason. What attracted the cameras, however, was not these laid-out bodies, but the tattoos etched on their foreheads.

"These are their numbers in concentration camps," he said to the blonde reporter who wanted her channel, by all means, to be the first to broadcast the interview. "I know neither their names nor their cities nor their villages. All I know is that they are my own people." What the blonde reporter could not fathom was why all those bodies were with one foot, one leg, or one eye.

"How else would two feet, two legs, and two eyes be a luxury?" he replied.

Requiem

"THURSDAY NIGHT in Garden Hall, Friday night in Tulip Inn, on such and such night in . . ." he scribbled in his little notebook. "To be an artist and a businessman takes its toll on you. But life goes on, and we will take our share of joy even during the war," he told the band that elected him its manager.

In the final concert, the band played one tune all night long, while right behind the mike stood a larger-than-life picture of the band's singer, in his black eyeglasses, waving his hand and saluting his audience. Black coffee was served to everyone present.

There was something they knew, but all secretly agreed to a conspiracy of silence, just listening to the martyr's requiem.

Takseem Square Singer

"THIS RED SCARF is mom's gift on my graduation from the Higher Institute of Music," he said by way of giving himself a breather. Pointing to a watch he was wearing, he added, "And this watch is the first one I wore. It was when I joined the National Symphony."

She laughed and said, "Must you remind me of the watch I stole from my father's locker? By the way, he knew but pretended to have lost it so that my mother would stop looking for it!"

"With your violin, you uplift our souls to heaven," commented a Turkish young man in Takseem Square, Istanbul, speaking through his Arab interpreter and girlfriend. Serenading his audience with old songs, passersby danced with matchless ecstasy, and while they were throwing banknotes in his violin case, his soul soared south like a woman seer milling around the gates of old Damascus.

He recalled all those who ran away from their homeland to sing their pain in metro stations or airport transit lounges.

Defense

"Your honor, what's the crime of this young gentleman standing before you? He is a true blood who gave first aid to the injured, prompted by nothing but the dictates of his free conscience, and even paid for the medication out of his own pocket, risked his own life under bombardment fire just to make good his oath, Sir.

"Fellow counselor, allow me to finish my defense, please," he said, pointing to the void. These were bits and pieces from the defense of the Counselor, as he has been known since he joined the bar twenty years ago. The young lawyer, standing next to him, helps him carry his briefcase which he brings with him every day at exactly the same time he unfailingly kept ever since he started his practice twenty years ago in the now destroyed Justice Street.

Need I tell you of the crowds of passersby gathered in front of the Court of Justice, closed for the last two years in our city? While his wife was balancing his lawyer's robe on his shoulders in order not to reveal what's underneath, it began to rain. Streamlets formed and washed people's faces, and his defense has not yet been completed.

The Wooden Horse

Her Russian coach used to say of her, "Her body is like a piece of music, which she controls like a tyrannical ruler. On the display mat, she walks like a Byzantine icon." He also nicknamed her Daria in honor of Russian gymnast Daria Kondakova.

"I want a gymnastic leg, Doc!" Now that's what *she* said to the therapist supervising her rehabilitation with a prosthetic limb. He hid his smile by immersing himself in reading her medical reports.

"I wish the plane delayed its bombardment that night just a little," she mused in self-pity. "Or I exercised a little longer in the basement of that sports center."

Wishing to check her full recovery, the psychotherapist asked her, laughing, "Can you do your rhythmic gymnastics in this wonderful hall? It's not like those miserable ones in your country, you know."

"Perhaps, I can," she answered the fat therapist with a smirk, "if you cut the legs of this wooden horse and bring it closer to the floor."

The Surrealist

"IN OUR COUNTRY, mountains squat like dogs on their haunches in front of the sea. Some of their residents are pirates mounted on wooden horses, who roam the bays in search of ships loaded with pearls and slaves. In heaven, there is a hand with countless fingers, and a cloud exuding sorrow like the breast of a childless mother.

"That skull, through whose sockets the light travels, used to be a good singer and had its own private dreams. And the deep sunken dent in the forehead is still screaming. This tunnel might lead you to your own heart. You can't pour me, I, who was once a butterfly in the field, into a bottle of sin. That road leads nowhere, Mount Qasiyoun didn't bathe during the last *Eid*, and the pigeons of the Umayyad Mosque are looking for a passport. It is a warped light that which comes from the East, and the priest is a man of a proven criminal record."

I saw him opening the window of the room given to him in the refugee complex on the outskirts of Athens, and he was throwing those sheets I've just read to you.

I said, "Perhaps, they are only the preludes to novels or surrealist texts, or maybe just the confessions of man on the brink of madness."

White Carnations

A T THAT MOMENT, she wished she were just a little taller to be able to see him. She wanted to make the connection between his pure voice and image. She stood on the tip of her toes and hardly saw a strand of his hair, which he strove to push back in order not to block his view. This is the first time a demonstration had a taste other than that of revolution and freedom.

It was a long evening that reminded her of Imru'l Qays's night in his long suspended ode. Oh, those were good old days in the college of arts, our own love boat. A morning monologue over a cup of coffee.

He cut white carnations from all the houses in the neighborhood and sprinkled them with water. And just before the evening demonstration had started, he distributed them among the most enthusiastic participants. The last carnation was hers. She smiled only half a smile, and his face blushed. He tripped and nearly fell.

When the informants' bullets rained and hit the first row of the young demonstrators, a scream went up. Rushing to the source, she was able to make the connection between the pure voice and the elegant image of the long-haired man.

His blood had turned the white carnation into a bright red one, while she still clutched her white flower as bright as light.

An Entrepreneur

"MY FRIENDS, you can wait for your salary until the end of the month and waste your lives in government departments. You can also write poems in praise of your general directors, and don't forget to sing and dance conscientiously on the Leader's birthday."

Then he chuckled uproariously. He concluded his college valedictory speech, "As for me. . . " but the phrase was drowned amid the applause and screaming.

"I like gilded metal plaques," he told the interior designer who decorated his offices. He put "Entrepreneur" on his personal card.

"I can distribute food to fighters, bring them warm clothes, and make an accurate and austere budget. Aren't I an entrepreneur?" asked the young businessman-turned-fighter. "A former entrepreneur, I mean." He corrected himself. "C'est la guerre!"

Dying with Joy

H E WAS FOND OF HIS MILITARY PHOTOS. Here he is wearing the blue uniform of "Sky Eagles," and in this one he is wearing the white uniform of the Navy, and there he is in fatigues, the uniform of Task Forces.

Though he is an accomplished pianist—piano being his favorite instrument—he insists on saluting her, military style, after every tune he plays; and she would return the courtesy by sprinting towards him like a stray enamored gazelle.

"This young man is dying; his grade 3 tumor is spreading fast. Only a few days to live. To be exempted from military service." This was decided by the Army's Supreme Commission. It was his mother who, after several visits to the ranch of her old friend on the west coast, had those reports contrived. And while she distributed sweets and danced, her son was dying with joy. "It's still a sort of death, somehow," he kept saying to his girlfriend, while his mother, still ecstatic with her triumph, said, "It's a dirty war!"

At the Last Checkpoint

At the last checkpoint, a paratrooper in military fatigues and Adidas shoes examined the driver's face and told him to get off the bus. Scared, the driver asked, "Sir, what's my charge? What have I done wrong? I am just a simple bus driver."

"I just don't like your face."

The passengers held their breath and hoped that this, too, would pass and they would eventually get to their destination in spite of the unexpected delays.

The paratrooper asked the scared driver, "Who's your god, you shithead?"

"He is mine and yours, Sir. I worship the same God as you do, Sir."

"Then let this god of yours save you from me."

He then ordered the bus driver to face a nearby wall. The sun was dazzling. With all his might he assaulted the driver with the butt of his AK-47. The assault was so violent that the assailant tripped and accidentally pulled the trigger and killed himself.

The driver and his passengers resumed their much interrupted journey.

From the Translator

THE WORK OF A TRANSLATOR has often been compared, for better or worse, to midwifery. The case could not be truer than in this work. Indeed, I was involved in it since its conception. My friend, Dr Musa Rahum Abbas, originally began publishing some of these tales on his Facebook page. I immediately saw the potential and the intense literary merit in these tales that capture the various aspects, often neglected in the media, of the unfolding Syrian tragedy.

I encouraged him to write more of these condensed sketches, and promised that if he were to write a total of 100, I would translate them into English. We both regarded this collaborative effort—by no means a crude piece of political propaganda—as the least we could do to draw attention to the ongoing suffering of individuals from all walks of Syrian life. A few months later, Musa Abbas finished the promised collection.

Soon after the publication of the original in Amman, I sounded my friend and colleague Dr Sanna Dhahir, Dean of the College of Science and Humanities at Effat University, about collaborating on the translation. She was more than happy to oblige. The tales she translated are 86 through 100.

Tale 101 was neither in the Arabic original nor included, as an afterthought, by the author for this translation. It is my own contribution, though it is not an original piece of creativity. The story it tells is based on a real incident that took place in Harasta, a suburb of Damascus.

What mattered to me the most was not that it was just another real example of the whimsical atrocities committed by pro-Assad, paramilitary hooligans against helpless, innocent civilians, but its finale loomed as an example of much needed poetic justice. It opened a window of hope.

"We are doomed to hope," said Syria's erstwhile best known dramatist Saadalla Wannous, author of the Message of World Theatre Day 1996, sent from his deathbed. If the whole world lets us down—as it has done over the last six years—divine justice won't! We desperately need to hang onto any glimmer of hope, however distant.

Dr Dharir and I would like to extend our thanks for their proofing, editing, and other assistance to Dr Marream Krollos of Effat University, Fatimetou Sidiya and Jahla Aldeeb.

Musa Al-Halool
Taif, Saudi Arabia
January 2022

Cune Press

Cune Press was founded in 1994 to publish thoughtful writing of public importance. Our name is derived from "cuneiform." (In Latin *cuni* means "wedge.")

In the ancient Near East the development of cuneiform script—simpler and more adaptable than hieroglyphics—enabled a large class of merchants and landowners to become literate. Clay tablets inscribed with wedge-shaped stylus marks made possible a broad inter-meshing of individual efforts in trade and commerce.

Cuneiform enabled scholarship to exist, art to flower, and created what historians define as the world's first civilization. When the Phoenicians developed their sound-based alphabet, they expressed it in cuneiform.

The idea of Cune Press is the democratization of learning, the faith that rarefied ideas—pulled from dusty pedestals and displayed in the streets—can transform the lives of ordinary people. And it is the conviction that ordinary people, trusted with the most precious gifts of civilization, will give our culture elasticity and depth—a necessity if we are to survive in a time of rapid change.

 Aswat: Voices from a Small Planet (a series from Cune Press)

Looking Both Ways	Pauline Kaldas
Stage Warriors	Sarah Imes Borden
Stories My Father Told Me	Helen Zughraib

Syria Crossroads (a series from Cune Press)

Visit the Old City of Aleppo	Khaldoun Fansa
The Dusk Visitor	Musa Al-Halool
Steel & Silk	Sami Moubayed
The Road from Damascus	Scott C. Davis
A Pen of Damascus Steel	Ali Ferzat
White Carnations	Musa Rahum Abbas
Nietzsche Awakens!	Farid Younes
The Passionate Spies	John Harte
Stories of My Father	Helen and Elia Zughaib

Bridge Between the Cultures (a series from Cune Press)

Confessions of a Knight Errant	Gretchen McCullough
Afghanistan & Beyond	Linda Sartor
Apartheid is a Crime	Mats Svensson
Congo Prophet	Frederic Hunter
Arab Boy Delivered	Paul Aziz Zarou

⟪ꝺ⟫Cune Cune Press: www.cunepress.com

The Author

Musa Rahum Abbas is revered in the Arab world as a poet, fiction writer, and academic. He is a native of Raqqa, Syria (recently the headquarters of ISIS in Syria and later destroyed by US bombing). Abbas has lived for many years in Saudi Arabia where he works as a scholar and writer. He is the author of a volume of poetry *(al-Afilun),* a novel *(Bilan),* and a collection of short stories *(Buruq Ala Thuqub Sawda). White Carnations* is his debut work in English.

The Translators

Musa Al-Halool, who earned his PhD in Comparative Literature from the Pennsylvania State University in 1995, is a Syrian academic, short story writer, and literary translator with over forty books to his name. He is currently Professor of English and Comparative Literature at Taif University, Saudi Arabia.

Sanna Dhahir is an Iraqi-Canadian with a PhD in English literature from the University of New Brunswick, Canada. She has published several articles on post-colonial and Arabic literature. She is also a literary translator, and her latest translation, Badriyya Al-Bishr's *Hind Wa-l'skar,* is being published by the Center for Middle Eastern Studies, University of Texas Press. She has served as Associate Professor of English and Dean of the College of Science and Humanities at Effat University, Saudi Arabia.

CPSIA information can be obtained
at www.ICGtesting.com
Printed in the USA
JSHW041952030322
23395JS00013B/13